GIFT OF THE EARTH

by

PACHITA CRESPI

Charles Scribner's Sons

New York   1946

GIFT OF THE EARTH

It was the night before Christmas. Everything was very still in the little hut made of straw and shaped like a beehive. The bright colored macaw had ceased his shrill calls. The green parrot, who had chattered all day long, was asleep on his perch over the doorway with his head tucked under his wing. Before the open stove a big brown pig lay asleep on the earthen floor. Outside in the patio the rooster and his eight hens were perched high on the branches of the coffee bush, safe from the prowling fox.

Three black eyed *chiquitas* (little girls) Claudia, Márgara, Teresa and Bienvenido their brother, whose name meant Welcome, were all lying on a bunk made of bamboo sticks covered with a mattress of large dry leaves from the tall plantain. To save their clothes from being torn and worn out too quickly, they had played all day naked under the hot tropical sun. Now, to protect them from the cold mountain air, they were clothed for the night in dresses which their mother, Antonia, had made of flour sacks. They were sleeping so soundly that they were not disturbed by the pale glow of the candle that burned in the neck of a bottle.

Antonia and José, the parents of the *chiquitas* were squatting on the floor of the hut. They were build- ing the manger, as they did  every Christmas Eve. Antonia carefully placed a tiny figure of the Christ Child in a crib filled with straw. José placed the Virgin and St. Joseph on either side of the crib. Not a word was spoken between them, but when dark eyes met, each knew the other was sad because they were unable to fulfill their little girls' great wish for a doll. The *chiquitas* had been pray- ing that the Christ Child might bring them a doll on Christmas Day. But José and Antonia knew that what little money they had saved would have to be used for buying more seeds to replant their field with rice, corn, black beans, and sugar-cane so that they would have enough to eat.

When the manger was finished, José took off his big straw hat and his belt, from which hung his long machete knife, and rolled into the bunk, Antonia untied her cotton apron strings and was ready for bed, too.

Early the next morning, before the *chiquitas* awoke, José went out to work in his field. He was digging into the rich black earth to plant more seeds when suddenly his shovel hit something hard. At first he thought it was a rock, so he squatted down and tried to remove it with his strong, brown fingers. As he worked, his hands began to tremble with excitement, for he saw that the rock was really a red clay doll. He passed a hand over his unbelieving eyes and looked again, pushed back his hat and scratched his black mop of hair. Yes, there was a real DOLL in the deep hollow he had dug! He lifted it out and carried it carefully to the hut.

José's big eyes were shining as he placed the doll in Antonia's hands. "From where does it come?" she whispered.

The
Manger

"I myself don't know, Antonia. It came out of the earth."

"It must be a gift from Heaven," she replied, and hurriedly placed it at the foot of the manger so that when the *chiquitas* woke up and ran there to see what the Christ Child had brought them for Christmas, they would find the doll awaiting them.

"The Christ Child has come!" "The Christ Child has come!" the *chiquitas* shouted when they awakened.

Without taking off the white cotton dresses they had slept in, they ran to the manger to see if the Christ Child had answered their prayer. And there was the doll! Even the green

parrot on his perch flapped his wings excitedly, stretched his neck and cackled along, imitating the *chiquitas* as they cried, "Papa, Mama,  Look! The Christ Child has not forgotten us!"

The little girls squatted on the floor at the foot of the manger, admiring the doll.

"See," Claudia pointed, "she has waves of clay for hair!"

"And a flat nose," cried Teresa, "like Bienvenido!"

Márgara said, "She has big ears just like Papa!"

José and Antonia and Bienvenido joined the noisy group. The rooster strutted in with his eight hens, and the big brown pig sniffed and grunted curiously around the doll.

"Papa! Papa!" cried the *chiquitas* desperately, "the rooster and the hens and the pigs are going to break our doll!"

José quickly chased the creatures out of

the hut, waving his big *sombrero* at them.
"Don't worry, *chiquitas*," he said, "I shall make
a box for the doll and then you can hang her
in the box on the wall so that the pig and the
rooster and the hens won't be able to knock
her over."

Antonia chimed in, "And I shall make a
little dress for her from a flour sack to keep
her warm at night."

The *chiquitas* were delighted. "Mama!
Mama! She can go without clothes in the day
like us, and play in the sun with us!" Márgara
said.

That night the doll slept in her box on the wall safe from the pig and the rooster and the chickens.

Next morning, bright and early, the *chiquitas* pulled off their white cotton dresses, took the doll from her box and sat on their four-legged stools around the table. Antonia served them strong black coffee in green tin cups. The *chiquitas* sweetened their coffee with heaping teaspoons full of brown sugar and munched their round cornmeal cakes. Breakfast over, the *chiquitas* ran out of the door of the straw hut and played with their doll all morning long in the shade of the spreading plantain. José left for the village and the little girls asked him to bring back a green tin cup for the doll so that she, too, could have coffee with them.

Ten o'clock was lunch time. Antonia appeared in the doorway calling: "Claudia, Teresa, Márgara! Come in to eat!"

The *chiquitas* ran into the hut. Antonia served them heaping portions of fried rice on tin plates, with fried black beans and boiled plantains. Again they drank black coffee sweetened with lots of brown sugar. The doll sat on the table, and Bienvenido had a grand time crawling on the floor among the brown pig and the rooster and the eight white hens which feasted on the grains of rice and black beans that fell from the table onto the floor. After their meal the *chiquitas* went out to play again with their lovely clay doll.

At dinner time, four o'clock, Antonia served them fried rice, black beans, plantains and black coffee. José had returned from the village with a shiny, green tin cup for the doll, who sat with them at the table.

"See," Claudia said, holding the cup to the doll's lips. "She is drinking coffee with us!"

At bed time, the *chiquitas* put on their white cotton dresses. Then they put on the doll's white cotton dress which Antonia had made, and put her back into her box. Soon the *chiquitas* and Bienvenido were sound asleep on the wooden bunks.

Saturday was bath day, and the *chiquitas* took their doll with them down to the river. Here Antonia scrubbed the little girls, Bienvenido and herself with a cornhusk and black soap made from the fat of a pig. They dipped again and again into the clear, cool water of the river. They had no towels, so the *chiquitas*, their doll, Bienvenido and Antonia sat happily on the grass to let the warm tropical sun dry them off quickly.

Monday was washday. The *chiquitas* followed Antonia down to the river. Antonia waded to the middle of the river where she squatted on a large flat rock. The *chiquitas* squatted on the rock beside her and took turns watching Bienvenido so he would not fall off the rock into the water. Antonia washed her flowered skirt, her gayly colored blouses and aprons, José's striped pants and colored shirts, and the three white cotton dresses of the *chiquitas*. Claudia, Teresa and Márgara took turns washing the doll's white cotton dress until it was nice and clean. When all the clothes were washed and rinsed, Antonia spread them on the sweet smelling grass to dry. The little girls spread the doll's dress beside the other laundry.

Then Antonia said: "I am going to the house to cook your dinner. Claudia, Teresa and Márgara, you stay here to make sure that the rooster and the white chickens do not walk over the laundry and the brown pig does not

At
the River

come snooping around with his dirty brown snoot."

"Yes, Mama," the *chiquitas* said together, "we will see that the rooster and the white chickens and the brown pig do not soil your clothes."

While the *chiquitas* took care of the laundry for Antonia, they played happily with their doll. First Claudia would pretend she was combing the doll's thick black hair. Then Teresa tied a long blade of grass around the doll's head, making believe it was a green ribbon. Claudia pretended that the doll had not obeyed Antonia and let the rooster and the chickens and the pig soil the clothes. So Teresa turned the doll over to spank her, saying: "You are a bad doll. You are a bad doll." Just the way Antonia would spank the *chiquitas* when they had disobeyed. Soft-hearted Márgara wiped away the tears from the doll's eyes. Then Claudia, Teresa and Márgara kissed the doll and said: "I know you are going to be a good doll now," just as Antonia did after they had been punished.

The game was over. Antonia came to gather up the wash. She took Bienvenido in her arm and went back to the hut, followed by the three little girls. Teresa and Márgara each held the doll by an arm as if she were walking with them. Claudia carried the doll's clean white dress.

Many days passed for the happy little girls. They took turns in dressing the doll at night and undressing her in the morning.

One day an elegant gentleman from the city, riding on a fine chestnut horse, stopped

 at the straw hut. He was on his way to his ranch in the mountains. He tied the horse up in the shade of the long, spreading plantain leaves and stepped to the open door of the hut, asking for a drink of water.

Antonia graciously filled a thin round gourd with cool spring water from the clay jar and gave him a piece of *dulce* (brown sugar).

"Thank you Señora," said the stranger as the green parrot, from his perch screamed, "Thank you Señora!" The Señor sipped the water and sucked the sugar. Suddenly his eyes were drawn to the doll in the box on the wall, so he walked over to examine it more closely.

"And the little figure, Señora," he asked, "where did you get it?"

"My husband found it in the earth, Señor," Antonia replied. "It was a gift from the earth at Christmas time."

Just then José walked into the hut and the

man turned to him. "I will give you ten dollars for this figure," said the *Señor*, though he really did not know its value. José needed money very badly, but when he saw the anxious eyes of his *chiquitas* peeping around the doorway, he mumbled, "This doll is not for sale, *Señor*."

A month went by and another stranger came to the door. This one was tall and fair.

"*Buenas noches* (good evening)," he said. "*Buenas noches! Buenas noches!*" mimicked the green parrot.

Speaking to José the stranger said, "I have lost my way. Will you show me the road to the airport?"

"Si, si, Señor," replied José. "Yes, I will show you the way."

At that moment the stranger's eyes fell on the doll. He walked over to the box and picked her up. The *chiquitas* followed him with their round eyes to see what he was doing to their doll. Carefully the stranger examined her. Then he scratched her with the nail of his thumb and some of the clay fell off. The *chiquitas* were horrified.

"Where did you get this figure?" the stranger asked.

José told him how he had found the doll in the earth on Christmas Day. "Well, you certainly had a lucky Christmas," answered the stranger. "Come here, I will show you something."

The family gathered around and he pointed to where he had scratched the doll. "See," he said, "she is made of solid gold!" They all stared in amazement.

"In my country, America," continued the stranger, "these dolls found in Indian graves are very valuable."

Antonia and José looked delighted, but the stranger saw tears in the eyes of the chiquitas,

so he said, "Don't worry, *chiquitas*, your doll will have a fine home in America."

Then he went on. "Her red coat of clay will be removed, and she will shine in golden splendor. She will live in a glass case in a large palace where guards will watch over her day and night to see that no one carries her away. And," he told them, "people will come from everywhere to admire her. Beneath her will be written how the Mayan Indians made her many years ago," he continued, "and how she became lost in the earth until your Papa discovered her in the field behind your house." But still the *chiquitas* looked sad.

Then the stranger promised them, "I shall send you three dolls—one for each of you—

from America." And at this the *chiquitas* smiled again. Seeing that they were quite happy now the stranger paid José well for the little Indian

*"Buenas
Noches Señor"*

doll. And again he went out into the dark.

The next morning, when the *chiquitas* awoke, the stranger had already left with the doll. Her box hung on the wall sad and empty.

The *chiquitas* could hardly swallow their coffee and their corn cakes. José, seeing that they were sad, said: "Come, I'll show you how to make a kite."

At the thought of a kite the *chiquitas* almost forgot the doll and jumped up and down with joy. In the shade of the spreading plantain they watched José make a kite. He took a long dry leaf from the ground and to its stem he tied a long string. "Come, *chiquitas*, to the top of the hill where the wind blows."

When they were at the top of the hill José ordered: "You, Claudia, who is the tallest, hold the end of the leaf in your right hand high above your head. You, Teresa, who has the longest legs, hold the end of this string. When Márgara says 'One, two, three' you, Claudia, let the leaf go and you, Teresa, run fast."

"One, two, three," counted Márgara. Claudia let the leaf go, Teresa ran, and the leaf danced and whirled and flew high up into the air. The *chiquitas* were entranced and José, seeing that they were happy, left them to play and went back to plow his field.

But on Friday, market day, José would leave the straw hut at the break of dawn to go to the market in the village to sell bags of beans and rice and stalks of sugar-cane. For now his farm was yielding well, as he had money from the sale of the doll to buy seeds and have a big crop.

And on market day, the *chiquitas* would

always ask the same question: "Papa, do you think that the American has sent the dolls and that you will find them at the post office today?"

"If they are there I shall bring them to you." With this promise José would leave and the *chiquitas* would wait all day long at the door of the straw hut, their eyes fixed on the path, expecting José to come up with the three dolls. Many market days passed and no dolls appeared. A dozen times a day the *chiquitas* ran to Antonia and asked the same question over and over again.

"When will the dolls come? How will they come?"

"Our Costa Rica plane with its big silver wings will fly down from America with them."

"But when—" the *chiquitas* could not stop asking it.

Each time Antonia answered patiently, "Maybe they will come tomorrow."

But as the weeks passed and no dolls appeared, the *chiquitas* were sure that the American had forgotten them. Then one day José returned from a trip to  the village. He carried three long boxes. His eyes were shining as he entered the hut. The *chiquitas* ran to him. He smiled and handed Claudia one package, Márgara one package, and Teresa one package. "They came by today's plane," he said.

604440

Quickly the *chiquitas* squatted on the floor and hurriedly unwrapped their packages. José looked down at them smiling, "It was indeed a lucky Christmas for us, *chiquitas!*" For in each package was a beautiful doll.

"Qué linda! How beautiful!" said Claudia.

"Qué linda! How beautiful!" said Márgara.

"Qué linda! How beautiful!" said Teresa, holding her yellow-haired doll close in her arms.